Happy ♡ B[...]
Alex   Love Linda
   + Doug xxo

To my friend Mark
—*J. A.*

SIMON & SCHUSTER BOOKS FOR YOUNG READERS
An imprint of Simon & Schuster Children's Publishing Division
1230 Avenue of the Americas, New York, New York 10020
Text copyright © 2014 by Joanna Walsh
Illustrations copyright © 2014 by Giuditta Gaviraghi
Originally published in 2014 in Great Britain by Simon & Schuster UK Ltd.
All rights reserved, including the right of reproduction in whole or in part in any form.
SIMON & SCHUSTER BOOKS FOR YOUNG READERS is a trademark of Simon & Schuster, Inc.
For information about special discounts for bulk purchases, please contact Simon & Schuster
Special Sales at 1-866-506-1949 or business@simonandschuster.com.
The Simon & Schuster Speakers Bureau can bring authors to your live event. For more information or to book an event,
contact the Simon & Schuster Speakers Bureau at 1-866-248-3049 or visit our website at www.simonspeakers.com.
Book design by Tom Daly
The text for this book is set in Artcraft URW T.
Manufactured in China
0316 SUK
2 4 6 8 10 9 7 5 3
CIP data for this book is available from the Library of Congress.
ISBN 978-1-4814-6266-2
ISBN 978-1-4814-6267-9 (eBook)

I Love Dad

Joanna Walsh

Illustrated by Judi Abbot

A Paula Wiseman Book
Simon & Schuster Books for Young Readers
New York London Toronto Sydney New Delhi

Nobody in the morning yawns as big as **Dad**.

Nobody snores so awesome.

Nobody's kisses are so bristly.
Nobody's stubble so
double-itchy.

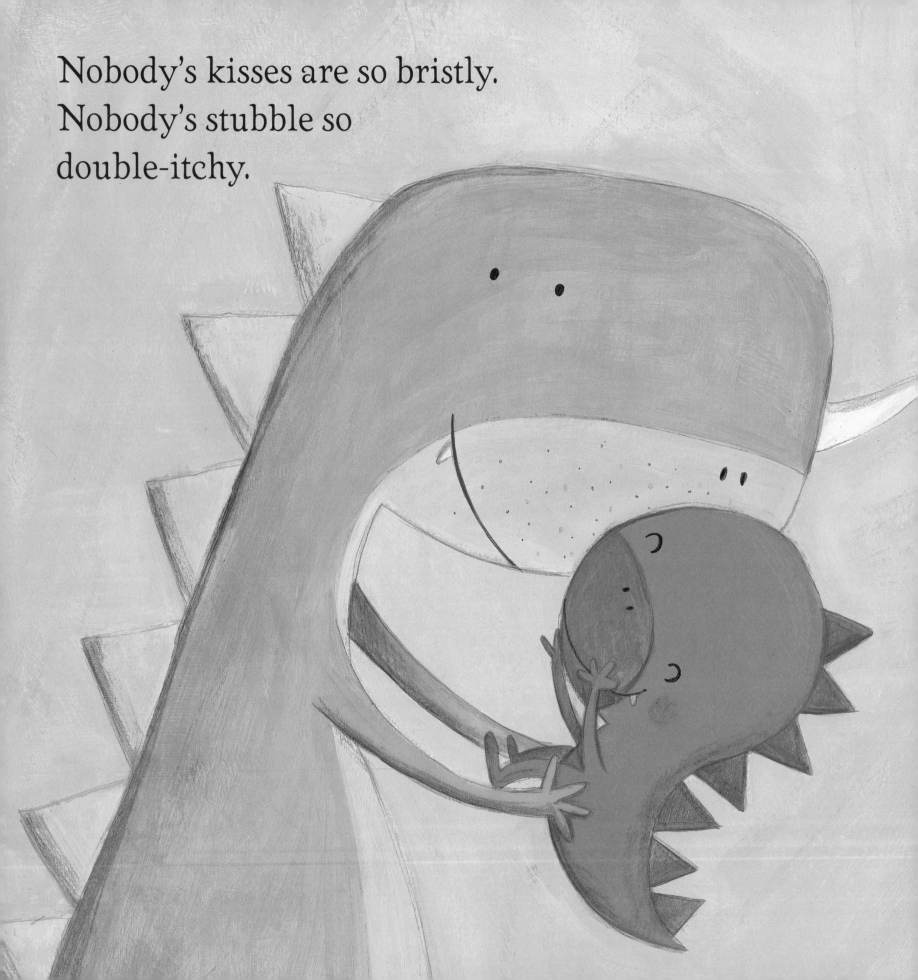

Who else could be so tickly,
trick so quickly?

No one else makes breakfast into a festival.
Dad throws the best morning party ever.

I'd never thought juice and cereal
really special.

Who'd have guessed it?

Who else gives me a feeling
of being as tall as
the ceiling?
Better go outside
where . . .

nobody's shoulders could be higher,
so near the sky for such
a lively ride.

Nobody's arms are
such an airplane,

nobody's foot a swing,

no one's knees such
a queasy trampoline.

Now, says **Dad**, let's get out our bikes,
pump up the tires until we burst for air!
A dab of grease,
some oil squirts here
and there.
No one was ever such a fixer-upper.

Dad on wheels!
Dad in the saddle
cycles faster than a bike will pedal . . . .

till we're
tired and then we
freewheel
downhill to home.

But, if it rains,
who else wakes up parades of toys
and makes them walk and speak?

Who gets out boards and cards
and chases pieces around?
A tiddlywink to finish first
and a card house
to tumble down.

Cooking with **Dad's** a laugh,
a blast, not half
a spoonful wasted.

Who loves to eat
hamburgers, spaghetti, pizza?

But who always *makesh shure*
I BRUSH MY *TEESH* ?

Who can make
a bedtime story so fantastic,
a lion's roar so enthusiastic,
a plastic man's
kung-fu kick
so slick?

And when the clock ticks around
to time for sleep,
I know tomorrow will
be full of things to do
with **Dad** again.